AMERICAN ADVENTURES

★ ★ ★

TROUBLED TIMES

The Great Depression

Grateful acknowledgment is made to the following for permission to reprint previously published material:

The Lucky Star by Judy Young, illustrated by Chris Ellison. Text copyright © 2008 by Judy Young. Illustrations copyright © 2008 by Chris Ellison. Originally published by Sleeping Bear Press, 2008.

Rudy Rides the Rails: A Depression Era Story by Dandi Daley Mackall, illustrated by Chris Ellison. Text copyright © 2007 by Dandi Daley Mackall. Illustrations copyright © 2007 by Chris Ellison. Originally published by Sleeping Bear Press, 2007.

Junk Man's Daughter by Sonia Levitin, illustrated by Guy Porfirio. Text copyright © 2007 by Sonia Levitin. Illustrations copyright © 2007 by Guy Porfirio. Originally published by Sleeping Bear Press, 2007.

—⁓—

Sleeping Bear Press™

2395 South Huron Parkway, Suite 200
Ann Arbor, MI 48104
www.sleepingbearpress.com

Printed and bound in the United States.

10 9 8 7 6 5 4 3 2

Library of Congress Cataloging-in-Publication Data • Young, Judy. • [Short stories. Selections] • Troubled times : the Great Depression / written by Judy Young, Dandi Daley Mackall, Sonia Levitin ; illustrated by Chris Ellison, Guy Porfirio. • pages cm. – (American adventures) • Summary: "Contains three stories focusing on America's Great Depression. In The Lucky Star a girl teaches her sister and other children to read after their school is closed. In Rudy Rides the Rails a boy embarks on a hobo's journey across the country. In Junk Man's Daughter, an immigrant family struggles financially until they start a new business"– Provided by publisher. • ISBN 978-1-58536-903-4 (paper back) • 1. Depressions–1929–Juvenile fiction. [1. Depressions–1929–Fiction. 2. United States–History–1919-1933–Fiction. 3. Short stories.] I. Mackall, Dandi Daley. II. Levitin, Sonia, 1934- III. Ellison, Chris, illustrator. IV. Porfirio, Guy, illustrator. V. Title. • PZ7.Y8664Tro 2014 • [Fic]–dc23 • 2013038494

TABLE OF CONTENTS

The Lucky Star

Judy Young
Illustrated by Chris Ellison

"We don't have much," Momma said, "but remember, there's always someone who is worse off than you are. So count your lucky stars that you've got what you've got."

Momma was always counting her lucky stars. Poppa was one of them, and Ruth and her little sister, Janie, too. Their little house was a star, and so were their clothes, the food on the table, and even the fact that they had a table.

Momma's sky was filled with stars. On summer nights sitting on the porch steps, she would point up to the sky and say, "See that lucky star twinkling there? That one's for the breeze that kept the house cool today. And that one over there," she said, pointing in a different direction, "I'm counting that one for the shoes the neighbor gave you."

Ruth looked down at her feet and the old brown leather shoes. They were scuffed and creased, and the bottoms were nearly worn through. Twine laced through the eyes instead of shoelaces.

When the neighbor handed them to Ruth to try on, Momma said, "Count your lucky stars they are too big for you. You won't grow out of them for a long time."

Ruth didn't see Momma's stars. Her sky was big and dark, pitch black. For Ruth, there were no lucky stars shining down on them. Ruth was ten years old and was supposed to be going into the fifth grade. But it was 1933 and the Great Depression had swept the nation. Millions of people were out of work. Millions of families had very little money for food and clothes, and there was nothing left for treats.

September was just a week away when Ruth found out that school was a treat. The town could not afford to pay teachers or keep the school building lit and warm. Ruth would not be going to fifth grade.

"Count your lucky stars," said Momma, "that you were the star pupil in last spring's spelling bee."

Ruth looked at the collection of big red books with *The Book of Knowledge* written on the spines in shiny gold letters. They sat in their place on the shelf above her bed. Poppa had built that shelf especially for the books. They were her prize for spelling the word "perseverance."

Ruth knew all about perseverance. It meant to keep trying, even if things were hard. These times required a lot of perseverance.

Momma looked at the books, too. "You can use them to keep up with your studies," she continued, "until they can open the school again."

Ruth knew Momma was trying to cheer her up. Ruth loved school and Momma and Poppa were both proud of her.

"You are going to be our shining star," Ruth remembered Poppa saying. "You'll be the first in our family to graduate from high school.

"And Janie," he said, tickling Ruth's little sister, "it won't be long before you shine in school, too."

Ruth took one of the big red books off the shelf, trying to hold back tears. By doing well in school, she dreamed she would become the brightest star that glittered in Momma's sky. But now that light had been shut off.

How am I going to continue with my studies without a teacher? thought Ruth.

Janie reached out for the book and Ruth handed it to her. She watched as Janie curled up with it on the bed the two sisters shared.

Janie was supposed to start school this year. How would Janie learn to read?

Ruth looked at Momma and knew she was trying to think of another lucky star.

Ruth loved her mother, but she knew Momma would not be able to teach her. Momma had not gone to school and did not know how to read or write. Poppa could have been her teacher. He had been all the way through the sixth grade, but now he was not there to help.

That had been another star that had turned black.

Like millions of others, Poppa had lost his job.

He had worked at the lumberyard for years, but with the bad times people stopped building. Then the lumberyard owners could not afford to keep him. Both he and Momma found odd jobs to keep food on the table and a roof over their heads, but it had become harder and harder to do.

One day late last April, Poppa came home excited. He had a job! The Civilian Conservation Corps that President Roosevelt had developed to give young men jobs had hired Poppa because of his experience in the lumber industry. He would train and supervise young workers coming into the Corps.

The whole family was excited. Now they would not have to worry about becoming homeless like so many others.

But the good news brought sadness as well.

Although Poppa had a job, he would not be able to stay at home. He would be sent off to a work camp hundreds of miles away. Poppa said he didn't like the idea of being away from his family, but he would be paid thirty dollars a month and would send twenty-five of it home.

"Count your lucky stars," Momma said upon hearing the news. "With the money you make, there will still be a home for you to come back to."

But when Poppa went away, it felt like another star burned out of Ruth's sky.

Now Momma took the book from Janie, who had fallen asleep. She placed it back on the shelf and walked into the kitchen. Ruth followed her.

"I got a job," Momma said, "so I'll be gone every morning. You'll have to take care of Janie. Now I need to make biscuits for my lunch."

Ruth sat down at the table and watched as Momma mixed flour, shortening, water, and baking powder together. She sprinkled a little flour onto the table. As Momma kneaded the dough, Ruth ran her finger through the flour on the table. She was glad Momma found a job but it didn't cheer her up about the school closing.

While the biscuits were baking, Momma and Ruth walked out onto the porch and sat down on the steps.

The sun was going down and soon the sky would be filled with dots of light. They sat there quietly watching the orange and red sky. As the colors faded, the first tiny star began to twinkle ever so slightly. Momma pointed to it.

"See that star. That star is dim now, but watch it. It will grow brighter. That star is you, Ruth. You will be the lucky star for Janie. And don't worry. I know there's a lucky star out there for you, too. It will come with time."

With that, Momma kissed Ruth on the forehead and went into the house.

Ruth sat and looked at the star. As the sky darkened, it became brighter and brighter. Ruth thought about what Momma said and wondered what she meant. Once the sky had completely darkened, Ruth went in the house, too.

She lay down in bed next to Janie, watching the star through the window. Just as she was about to fall asleep, Momma's words whispered in her head. "You will be the lucky star for Janie."

Ruth looked at Janie sleeping peacefully beside her and smiled as an idea became as bright as a star in her mind.

Momma left early the next morning. Ruth helped Janie get dressed and then she started fixing biscuits for breakfast.

Just as Momma had done the night before, Ruth mixed flour, shortening, water, and baking powder together. She sprinkled a little flour onto the table and kneaded the dough. Then Ruth patted the dough flat with the palm of her hand. Janie used the lip of a jelly jar glass to cut out the round biscuits.

Ruth put the biscuits on a pan and into the oven to bake. Instead of cleaning the table, though, she lightly spread the leftover flour across the table, forming a thin layer of dust.

Janie watched Ruth curiously.

When the biscuits were done, the two girls ate them out on the front porch.

"You won't be able to start school this year," Ruth told Janie between bites, "because they closed it, but count your lucky stars you have me! I will be your teacher. Now, run along and bring back your friends. They need a lucky star, too. Tell their mommas they need to be here every day right after breakfast."

Soon Janie and her friends were gathered in the kitchen around the flour-covered table.

"I know nobody can afford pencils and paper, but count your lucky stars we have a little flour," announced Ruth.

Placing her hand over Janie's hand, Ruth guided Janie's finger through the flour.

"Go down and curve like an upside-down cane. That's the letter *J*," Ruth patiently told her.

"Now make an *A* like this," she said, guiding Janie's finger.

"Next, a zigzag for an *N*. The *I* is easy. Just make a straight line," Ruth said as she made Janie's finger slide through the flour.

"The *E* is last, like this," Ruth stated.

Ruth let go of Janie's hand. All the children looked at the letters formed in the flour.

"That's your name. *J-A-N-I-E*. Janie," Ruth exclaimed.

Ruth smiled at Janie and Janie smiled back.

Then Ruth helped each child write his or her own name in the flour. Soon, names were all over the table.

"Now go home and practice whenever your mommas make biscuits," Ruth told the children.

Momma's job lasted through the fall and winter and into the warm days of spring.

Each morning Ruth made biscuits and each morning the children came soon after breakfast. Ruth missed going to school but she loved teaching the children. They learned to write letters and numbers in the flour. They learned to read and write words and sentences.

Some days they sat on the porch. Using pebbles, Ruth taught them to count, add, and subtract. Then they went back in the house and learned to write math problems in the flour.

The best part of each day Ruth saved for the very last.

After their lessons, Ruth reached up to the shelf above her bed and pulled down one of the big red books. With the children gathered around her, she opened the book and read aloud. She read about history and people and places. She read about plants and animals, oceans and mountains. And she read about stars.

Each day, when she finished reading, Ruth turned to the page that showed a picture of a vast black sky dotted with twinkling stars, and each day she whispered quietly, "Count your lucky stars."

Spring was gone and now it was summertime. Almost a whole year had passed.

Ruth still wore the old brown shoes, although they fit a little better now. Poppa was still away from home, but the money

came every month. The school would still be closed in the fall but Janie and the other children were learning to read and write.

And now, at night when Ruth sat out on the porch steps with Momma, she saw how the sky was filled with stars.

FROM THE AUTHOR,
Judy Young

The Great Depression was an economic disaster that began in 1929 and lasted over a decade. Thousands of businesses shut down, leaving millions of people without jobs. Banks closed and people lost their savings. Many families lost their homes, unable to pay rent or mortgages. Items previously taken for granted became unaffordable luxuries as people struggled just to buy food and clothes.

Approximately 20,000 rural schools also closed during the Depression. Many more reduced the length of the school year to cut costs. In addition, numerous children dropped out of school to help their families earn money.

When writing *The Lucky Star*, I specifically chose the books won in the spelling bee and the main character's name so they would also be consistent with the time period. "Ruth" was one of the top ten girl names of the 1920s. I chose it in honor of my Aunt Ruth, who was a child during the Great Depression.

Rudy Rides
the Rails

Dandi Daley Mackall
Illustrated by Chris Ellison

Nineteen thirty-two was a time when America forgot how to smile. Drought turned the middle of the nation into "the Dustbowl." Corn and wheat prices fell so low that farmers left their crops in the field to rot. Banks ran out of money, and schools closed their doors. Fathers lost their jobs, and mothers had no food to put on the table for hungry children.

Rudy Phillips believed the whole world had changed.

And nobody had changed more than Rudy's pa.

Rudy tried to see around the line of men and boys winding ahead of him, clear to the boarded-up gate of the rubber plant. Everybody had hit on hard times.

Up ahead, people drifted out of line as word filtered down: "Nobody's hiring today."

Rudy shuffled home through the snow, wishing he had more than cardboard soles in his shoes. Pa was sitting on the porch step, looking as if all the hope had drained out of his bones. Rudy could remember when the front porch had been filled with Ma's singing and Pa's banjo playing. But when Pa lost his job, the music got lost, too.

"You gotta look out for you and yours, and nobody else." That's what Pa taught Rudy. But now Pa couldn't even take care of his own. Ma sneaked out to stand in line for cold beans and moldy cheese, while Rudy's little sisters waited at soup kitchen and mission back doors. Pa pretended not to know.

In the distance, Rudy heard the lonesome whistle of a train. Hundreds of teens no older than Rudy had hopped the B&O line out of Akron, Ohio, bound for lumbering forests in the north or fields ripe for harvesting to the west and south. They rode the rails to as far off as California, where orange trees grew in every yard and dreams had a chance of coming true.

"I'm going West," Rudy announced. When his pa didn't answer, Rudy pressed on. "I'll find work and send money home."

Ma cried and tried to talk him out of it. When she couldn't, she tied up a bundle, with a chunk of cheese, a loaf end of bread, and all she had, $2.10. Then she kissed her son good-bye. Rudy figured that even if he didn't strike it rich in California, there'd be one less mouth to feed.

Rudy hid in the weeds by the railroad yards. An outbound jerked onto the tracks like an iron snake, smoke puffing from its nostrils. A sliver of moonlight lit an open boxcar. Rudy jumped and grasped the grab iron to pull himself up. Then he rolled onto the boxcar floor. The whistle howled, and Rudy Phillips was on his way.

Inside the boxcar it was black as coal and twice as dusty. The floorboards shook like chattering teeth and smelled like sourdough gone bad. But as Rudy watched the yards grow smaller and smaller, he knew California was getting closer and closer.

Something stirred behind him. Rudy imagined rats the size of Ohio. He turned around to see a small circle of glowing red fire. Rudy wanted to jump from the train, but it swayed and bucked, and he couldn't stand up.

Rudy stared into the blackness until two figures took shape. One was bone thin and so tall he had to bend over. "Name's Fishbones," the man said. "This here's Boxcar Betty." Rudy saw now that the glowing circle was the tip of the old woman's cigar. She laughed, and Rudy thought of the witch's cackle in *Hansel and Gretel*. "You caught yourself a rattler, Sonny!" she declared.

It didn't take Rudy long to understand why the train was called a "rattler." It shook him like dice in a cup. Still, he was pretty sure that his insides would have been rattling, even if the train hadn't been. What if he'd made a mistake getting on this freight?

The biggest mistake of his life.

"What's your handle?" Fishbones asked.

"I'm Rudy," he answered. Pa's warning popped into his head: Look out for you and yours, and nobody else. Rudy curled up in the far corner of the boxcar and pretended to get some shut-eye. Finally, he did fall asleep, to the clickety clack and the sway of the track.

"Bulls ahead!"

Rudy woke with a start, surprised to see himself covered with newspaper.

"I'll take my Hoover blanket back now," Betty said, reaching for the paper.

Lots of folks blamed President Hoover for the Great Depression. Rudy handed back the Hoover blanket, wondering why she'd bothered covering him. "What kinda bulls?"

Fishbones pointed down the track to a handful of uniformed police, just waiting for them.

"Jump!" Fishbones hollered.

Rudy stared at the iron rails racing below. He closed his eyes and jumped. Two bulls were racing toward him.

Rudy took off running like lightning on fire.

When Rudy stopped to catch his breath, Fishbones appeared from behind a bush. "All clear," he said.

Boxcar Betty walked up. "Come on! I know a place we can get us a sitdown."

Rudy knew most hoboes went asking for food, but he could look out for himself. "Naw, I better git walkin'." He followed the tracks alone until he found a diner. Rudy ordered bacon, eggs, toast, and pancakes. With only a dollar of Ma's money left, he knew he had to find work.

Rudy tried seven places before he found a nickel flop that would let him sweep up for a dime a day. After six weeks in Chicago, "the Big Town," he had enough saved to send three dollars back home.

But the whistle was calling him. That night Rudy caught a freight on the fly, bound for the West.

In Freeport, Illinois, the train was met by farmers holding up signs that read, "Field Work! 10 cents an hour."

Rudy dug and planted from dawn until dark. When he thought he was too tired to lift the hoe one more time, he'd imagine what his ma would do when she got the money in the mail. He could picture her buying a chicken and surprising Pa and the girls with it. Or shoes. Maybe there'd be enough for her to get new shoes.

After a week in the fields, Rudy had spent half his wages filling the hole in his stomach. He sent the rest of the money home, then hopped a freight that was so full of hoboes he had to stand all the way to Dubuque, Iowa.

At a little whistle stop in Waterloo, when the other hoboes split up to panhandle near the tracks, Rudy was too hungry not to try it himself. He knocked at a cottage with flower beds. A woman came to the door, took one look at him, and slammed the door in his face. Rudy tried a big house, a run-down shack, and a house with a picket fence. Nobody gave him so much as a crust of bread.

When he got back to the boxcar, every other hobo was feasting. Rudy wondered how they could always pick the friendliest places. But he didn't ask. It was hard just looking out for himself.

In Britt, Iowa, a dozen hoboes got on and a dozen got off. Rudy spotted Fishbones and fell in a distance behind him, hoping Fishbones might lead him to a friendly house. Instead, Boxcar Betty showed up, and they ducked into the thick brush. Rudy followed farther and farther, winding through burnt-out cornfields, where dead stalks hung their empty heads. Rudy was afraid he'd never find his way out.

Rudy heard music. It had been so long since he'd heard singing that he stopped dead in his tracks. For a minute, he was back home on his own front porch, with Pa strumming and Ma singing, the smell of honeysuckle mixing with the promise of apple pie from the oven.

"Caught you!" A giant arm, thick as Rudy's leg, lifted him off the ground.

Fishbones came to the rescue. "Easy, Moose! This here's Ramblin' Rudy."

The man let go, and Rudy sprawled to the ground. "Welcome to the Jungle, Ramblin' Rudy!" he bellowed.

Rudy grinned. He finally had his very own handle, and he liked the sound of it.

Boxcar Betty led Rudy to a blazing bonfire and Rudy smelled something that made his mouth water.

"Mulligan stew," Betty explained. "But you got to put something in to take something out." She grinned, showing two missing teeth. "Wanna come with us to get grub?"

Rudy thought about Pa's warning to look out for himself. But he didn't want to get another door slammed in his face. His stomach ached for food he didn't know how to get. And that's all there was to it. Sometimes a boy did need somebody besides himself.

Rudy nodded. "I think I'd like that."

Fishbones led the way. They came to a nice, brick house, and Rudy could see a kindly-looking woman inside. "Here?"

Fishbones shook his head and pointed to a sign carved into the tree. It looked like a rectangle with a jagged line through it. "A bad-tempered woman," he said. Rudy didn't understand.

At the next house Boxcar Betty pointed out a sign scratched into the porch, a rectangle with a dot. "Danger," she whispered.

"Who left the signs?" Rudy asked, hurrying to keep up.

"Hoboes looking out for each other," Fishbones answered. He stopped and pointed to a big oak tree.

Rudy took a closer look. "It's a smiling cat."

Fishbones winked. "And it means we'll find kindness here."

Sure enough, a smiling woman came to the door. "Have a seat on the porch," she offered. "I'll see what I can find."

Back in front of the bonfire, Rudy felt pretty proud as he handed over cabbage, a turkey leg, and three potatoes for the pot. He wished his pa could have felt what he was feeling. Mulligan stew turned out to be the best meal Ramblin' Rudy had ever eaten, although he'd never tell Ma that. When nobody could eat another bite, Fishbones began a tune on his harmonica. Texas Slim beat on a frying pan. Pretty soon, Guitar Charlie and Banjo Bill joined in. Rudy closed his eyes and imagined he was back on his own front porch—before the world changed.

After that, Ramblin' Rudy learned from the hoboes he met. In Nebraska, when he tried to ride the "cowcatcher," the engine grate, cinders burned his eyes until "Shorty" Simms taught him to tie his bandana over his eyes. He rode the "blinds," the platform between connecting cars, through the Rockies and listened to "Preacher" Jones's stories about mountain men. Rudy climbed the roof to "catch the blue" through Utah and Nevada and wondered if the same sky, blue as his baby sister's eyes, reached all the way back to Akron.

Then one morning, Rudy woke to the sight of blue on blue—the Pacific Ocean stretching to the sky. He wished his folks could have seen it.

But as the U.P. chugged into the yards, Rudy could see that there were more hoboes than grains of sand in California. And all of them were looking for work.

It didn't take long for Rudy to discover California wasn't the place for him. If they'd had orange trees for everybody, they'd run out before Rudy got there. After odd-jobbing it for a spell, he knew what he wanted, what he needed—home. Before setting out, he got himself a good night's sleep at the Salvation Army. Come morning, Rudy Phillips would be heading home!

Rudy caught the eastbound and started working his way back. There were no smiling cats in the burning Arizona desert. Sunlight attacked through the slats of the boxcar and liked to bake him, until Frisco Fred showed him how to tie a wet bandana around his neck.

Rudy swept a saloon in Albuquerque, painted a church east of Dodge City, Kansas, washed windows, unloaded fruit, and chopped wood. He saved every penny. In the evenings, he found the sign of the smiling cat. He even got himself a sitdown in Kansas City from a woman who wasn't just looking out for herself.

Rudy had five dollars in his pocket when the B&O pulled into the Akron yards, past a long line outside the rubber plant. He ran all the way home, stopping only when he reached his front porch. Rudy could imagine music here.

Suddenly, he knew what he had to do. He got out his pocketknife, and into the porch he carved a smiling cat. Rudy stepped back and smiled at his hobo sign. From now on, folks who passed by would know they'd find kindness in the home of Ramblin' Rudy.

FROM THE AUTHOR,
Dandi Daley Mackall

On "Black Tuesday," October 29, 1929, the stock market crashed, and banks ran out of money. Millionaires lost millions. Average Americans lost everything they had. It was America's worst crisis since the Civil War and became known as the Great Depression. In Ohio, half of the workers in Cleveland lost jobs, 60% in Akron, and 80% in Toledo.

A quarter of a million teenagers left their homes to ride the rails as hoboes, in search of a better life. They were met with the same mixed reactions as our twenty-first-century homeless—ridicule and cruelty, along with the understanding and kindness of strangers.

My dad grew up close to the railroad tracks in Hamilton, Missouri. During the Depression, hoboes would stop and ask for a bite to eat.

My grandmother always gave them something. I met the real "Ramblin' Rudy," Rudy Phillips, in 2000. My story is a work of fiction, but I hope it captures Rudy's spirit and the spirit of American adventure lived by young Rudy and so many others during the Great Depression.

Junk Man's
Daughter

Sonia Levitin
Illustrated by Guy Porfirio

When we were still in the old country, every night Papa told my brothers and me about America. "You will see, Hanna," Papa said.

"There are streets of gold."

"Then everyone in America must be rich," I said. "Will we be rich, too?"

My little brothers, Manny and Morris, jumped up and down.

"Can we buy a bike? Will we have our own house and even a dog?"

Papa laughed and said, "We will see." He turned to Mama. "Bring plenty of empty sacks to America, so we can gather up the gold!"

"Of course," Mama said. "Plenty of sacks." And she went on knitting.

Relatives came to say goodbye. Grand-mother Lucy pinched my cheeks.

"In America you will be a famous dancer, Hanna," she said. "People will throw coins up onto the stage."

"Who needs coins in America?" I replied. "There are streets of gold."

"Quite so, Hanna," Grandmother said, wiping her eyes.

Uncle David pointed to Manny and Morris. "In America," he said, "these boys will be famous. Manny will be a doctor. Morris will be a lawyer. Don't worry about them."

"We don't worry," Papa said with a grin.

On the big day of leaving, everyone came to say good-bye. "Be well," they called. "We'll meet again some day!"

We traveled very far, very long, on a bus, a train, a ship.

At last we arrived in America.

I saw very tall buildings. I heard the grinding and groaning of cars and buses. People rushed and pushed against me. I wondered, *Were they all looking for gold?*

"Where is the gold, Papa?" I asked.

"We will keep our eyes open," Papa said. But his face looked stern and tired.

Papa rented a tiny apartment with two rooms and a fire escape. He bought three old chairs. We took turns sitting on them. My brothers and I slept on a mattress on the floor. We ate potatoes and onions, onions and potatoes.

Mama spent the whole day knitting shawls and sweaters to sell to people on the streets. Hardly anyone stopped to buy.

I wandered about the streets looking for gold. I peered behind trash bins. I bent down and traced the cracks in the sidewalk with my finger. I looked along the trolley tracks and behind the peddlers' carts in the alleys. There was no gold anywhere.

Papa needed work. Back home he was a teacher. But here in America there were teachers enough. Besides, Papa did not speak English. Winter came and we were cold. Even the scarves and sweaters that Mama knitted did not keep us warm.

Papa walked round and round, his head down. "What can we do?" he said. "We need food and coal. The children need shoes."

Mama boiled water for tea. "Be patient, Abram," she said. "Things will get better."

I went to him and shouted, "You lied to us, Papa! Where are the streets of gold?"

Papa jumped up. "I lied? How can you say this to your papa?"

I told him angrily, "I have looked everywhere, and there is no gold."

That night Papa and Mama talked for a long time. I heard Papa say, "Maybe we should go back to the old country."

"No," Mama said. "This is our home now. We will find a way. We must keep our eyes open."

The next day it snowed. Papa said, "I will walk with you to school, children. I can keep you warm under my coat."

Manny and Morris and I put on the caps and mittens and sweaters that Mama had knitted. We set out, trying to fit under

Papa's coat. I felt Papa shivering, and he did not look at me.

I will never forget that day, the icy wind, the thundering clouds. My hands and feet had no feeling in them.

We walked on and on, on and on. Once Papa sighed. Then he was silent.

But something changed. First the clouds opened. A ray of sun broke through. It shone upon the streets, slick with ice, spreading a soft, golden light.

"Look, Papa!" I cried. "You were right. See, the streets are of gold."

"Oh, Hanna," Papa said sadly. "I am so sorry. You were right before. I lied. There is no gold."

Just then something winked out from the slush and snow. I bent down quickly. It might be a penny or even a nickel! I picked up the shiny thing, and with my mitten scraped off the snow. Oh, it was only a bottle top. I cried out in a terrible voice, "It's nothing, nothing but junk!"

But Manny and Morris began digging through the snow, finding things. They found a bottle, then two more.

Papa rushed over. He laughed and clapped his hands together. "Bottles bring money!" he said. "Are there more?"

We dug through the snow, and soon we had gathered a pile of things—milk bottles, soda bottles, tin cans, bent nails, rusty knives and spoons, an old pot with no handle. Papa got a crate from a trash bin to put everything inside.

"We'll hurry to school now," Papa said. "This afternoon we will collect more. Oh, Hanna, we are saved."

Later that day Papa went out. When he came back, coins jingled in his pocket.

Mama looked up from her knitting. "So, you are going into business, Abram?"

"We," said Papa, smiling at my brothers and me. "It is a family matter."

So it began. Every afternoon my brothers and I went with Papa to find all the things that people threw away. We filled bags and boxes and carried everything home. The junk filled our small rooms and spilled out into the hall.

Mama stopped knitting. "We must sort everything," she said. Glass went into one box, metal into another, and paper and rags into another. Bottles went to the glass factory. The paper mill bought paper and rags. Tin cans were brought to the metal shop. We worked late into the night. My back hurt from bending. My hands were black with dirt. But we were making money. Every evening Papa put more coins into the large jar on the kitchen counter.

At school I was tired. The teacher called me to her desk. "Hanna, why don't you go to bed earlier? You are falling asleep in class."

I learned to keep my eyes open wide to make myself stay awake. After school I finished my homework quickly, so that I would be ready to go to work.

By now Papa had bought a wagon. My brothers and I took turns pulling the wagon through the streets. We looked for treasure in the gutter, at the docks, along the railroad tracks. Farther and farther we walked, pulling our wagon home, piled high with junk.

One afternoon three girls from school saw me. One girl wore a coat with a little fur collar. They all had boots and gloves. They pointed and called out, "Junk man's girl! Look at the dirty junk man's girl!"

I turned away. I would not let them see my tears. That day I found a broken silver cup. Papa did not sell it. "This is yours, Hanna," Papa said. "We are partners, after all. Ours is a family business."

When the jar in the kitchen was full, Papa went to the bank and opened a bank account. A little book showed our deposits, week by week. Papa rented a shed to keep all the junk we collected. We spent more time in that shed than we did at home.

Soon the wagon was too small. Papa traded it for a pushcart. And when the cart was not enough, Papa bought a truck. Slivers of old red paint showed under the rust and the grime. One door had no handle. But it was ours, and we danced around it, clapping our hands.

The very next day Papa said we would do no work at all. He took the truck away. Much later he called to us, "Come outside! Come and see!"

There it was, our shining red truck with brand new tires, and on the side, painted in large, golden letters were the words, ABRAM & FAMILY.

"Papa, we are rich!"

"That's how it is in America," said Papa.

"Streets of gold," Mama and I said, both together, laughing.

And that's how it was when we came to America long ago.

FROM THE AUTHOR,
Sonia Levitin

Junk Man's Daughter was inspired by real people who came to America looking for gold. They saw no gold in the streets. So they had to find other ways to make money. One way was to collect junk and to sell it for cash. Some immigrants did this. They would push a cart through the streets, calling out, "Bottles and rags! Old bottles and rags!" Sometimes the business grew to include broken pots and old stoves that could be changed into useful items. Today we call this recycling. Being a junk man or a junk man's daughter was not a glamorous occupation. But after years of hard work, some families became very wealthy.

Today large companies recycle all kinds of products, from tires to plastic goods, old appliances and computers, with factories all over the world. And it all started with junk.

Judy Young is an award-winning author of children's fiction, nonfiction, and poetry. Her other books include *A Book for Black-Eyed Susan* and *Tuki and Moka: The Tale of Two Tamarins*. Judy lives near Springfield, Missouri.

Dandi Daley Mackall met the real "Ramblin' Rudy," Rudy Phillips, in 2000. A prolific author and conference speaker, Dandi's other books include *A Girl Named Dan* and *The Legend of Ohio*. She lives in Ohio.

Sonia Levitin is the award-winning author of more than 40 books for children, teens, and adults. She and her family endow the Once Upon a World Children's Book Award. Sonia lives in southern California.

Chris Ellison has illustrated both children's picture books and adult fiction for nearly 20 years. His books include *The Lucky Star* and *Let Them Play* (a 2006 Notable Social Studies Trade Book for Young People). Chris lives in Mississippi.

Guy Porfirio graduated from the Academy of Art in Chicago and attended the School of Visual Arts in New York City. He has illustrated numerous children's books, including *Grandpa's Little One*, and lives in Arizona.